EA 0750 250305 9001

Dun Laoghaire-Rathdown Libraries
STILLORGAN LIBRARY
Inv/07 : L361J   Price E7.41
Title: Danny and the Sea of
Class: JF

D0318611

BAINTE DEN STOC

DÚN LAOGHAIRE-RATHDOWN COUNTY LIBRARY STOCK

WITHDRAWN FROM

- la na
deirea

Text copyright © David Clayton 1996
Illustrations copyright © Stephen Player 1996

First published in Great Britain in 1996,
and reprinted in 1998 by Macdonald
Young Books

Reprinted in 2006 by Wayland,
an imprint of Hachette Children's Books

The right of David Clayton to be identified as
the author and Stephen Player the illustrator of
this Work has been asserted by them in
accordance with the Copyright, Designs and
Patents Act 1988

Printed in China

All rights reserved. Apart from any use permitted
under UK copyright law, this publication may
only be reproduced, stored or transmitted, in any
form, or by any means with prior permission in
writing of the publishers or in the case of
reprographic production in accordance with the
terms of licences issued by the Copyright
Licensing Agency.

British Library Cataloguing in Publication Data
available

ISBN-10: 0 7502 5030 5
ISBN-13: 978 0 7502 5030 6

Wayland
an imprint of Hachette Children's Books
338 Euston Road, London NW1 3BH

DAVID CLAYTON

DANNY AND THE SEA OF DARKNESS

Illustrated by Stephen Player

WAYLAND

Chapter One

One summer night, not very long ago, I woke up feeling strange. It was hot when I went to sleep. But when I woke up my room was icy cold.

Outside, waves were booming and hissing. Trouble was, we live fifty miles from the nearest beach!

I was scared but I wasn't going to rush off to my mum like a baby, was I?

So I stayed put. My legs shook like jellyfish. There is *no sea* outside the window, I told myself. NO SEA, DANNY! FORGET IT!

Then *Crunch!* Another wave shook the house.

I shut my eyes and felt as if I was falling, down and down and down a great black hole until ... thud! I was back in bed.

Phew! I thought.

Another bad dream!

I decided to read for a bit. Put my hand out for my bedside lamp and – no lamp!

What is this? I thought. My sister Marie's idea of a *joke*?

But, as I slowly opened my eyes, I saw that everything had changed.

This isn't *my room* I thought.

Then *Whoomph!* I heard the sea again. Slowly I walked across to the window. Outside, there *should* have been our garden. But *No*!

Outside *this* window, there was just the salty sea, fizzing and foaming. I could smell it, taste it in the air.

It can't be true, I thought. You *can't* go to sleep in one place and wake up somewhere else! It was crazy. I jumped back in bed under the covers.

WHAM! An old, bearded man with a candle came barging into the room.

"Five o'clock, Michael," he snapped. "Move yourself, lad. There's work to be done!"

Michael? Who was Michael? *I'm* Danny! I thought. But I didn't say anything, the man looked so scary.

I didn't move to start with.

"By heck!" snarled the old chap. "I'll give you a good hiding if we miss the tide! I won't have any grandson of mine sleeping all day!" And out he stormed again.

Grandson? Sleeping all day? It was five o'clock in the morning!

One candle lit the room. That's all. There was no carpet, no curtains or wallpaper.

But there *was* a smell. This came from a
pile of stuff on the floor. There were
leather boots, an oilskin and long woollen
socks – all wet and salty and stinky.

Soon, heavy steps
were bumping up
the stairs again.

Time to get dressed, quick! Good job I did too!

For, CRUNCH! the door flew open. There was the grizzly grandad again.

"Up, eh? Come on – three hours out fishing on Reeper Bank, *then* we'll eat."

Was I dreaming?

No! The tough fisherman gave me a shove. That was real enough. And the first thing I saw outside was *very* real.

In front of us was the great, dark sea roaring like thunder. Waves as tall as houses fell over the boats.

I can't go out there! I thought. I won't last five minutes in that. But I had to.

I tried to hold the rope fixed to his boat but it was hopeless.

"Come on, lad! Hang on to it!" yelled the grandad.

WHAM! One wave and I was out.

When I bobbed up, the boat swung side on to the tide. Foam crashed into my face.

"YAAAAAH!" I yelled, grabbing an oar, eyes closed.

Strong hands pulled me on board.

Then, we were out there, whizzing like a waltzer on a fair.

"Pull, pull!" growled the old fisherman. "You're a man now!"

A *man*! I'm not a man! I'm only a kid!
I thought. But I still pulled like mad on
the oars.

"I'm scared! I'm scared!" I yelled.
But in reply, a big fist hit me in
the back.

"Pull, pull, boy! Reeper
Rocks ahead! … Michael!
Come on! Michael … God
help us!"

HISSSSSS! *Kerrunch! Too late.*

The rocks were chewing us up with their stony teeth, gobbling us down like a great shark.

"AAAAAAAAAAAH!" I cried as the boat flipped me out again.

There was time for only one breath. Then WHOOSH! I was under, oar and all.

In a few seconds, first my legs, then my arms went stiff as wood.

Hang on, Danny! *Hang on!* I told myself. Don't let go!

But slowly, slowly, the oar was slipping away.

"HEY!" said a loud voice. "Are you going to be in there *all morning*?"

Marie! That was my sister, Marie! What was she doing in the sea?

Marie's voice boomed again.

"I use the bathroom too, you know!" she went on.

Suddenly it hit me.

I wasn't in the sea any more. I stared at my white fingers. I was gripping the towel rail not an oar.

I had a good look at the mirror. Straggly red hair, white face covered in soapy water. Yes, that was me.

Marie was not happy.

"What's *going on* in there? Have you fallen down the plughole or something?"

I undid the door and stood out of her way.

"What *were* you doing? And what on earth were you shouting about?" she yelled as she raced in. "You're all at sea this morning!"

Chapter Two

When Marie said "all at sea", I didn't find it funny at all. The dark sea had gone away, but it could come back again.

If I go back to being Michael, I *will* drown! I thought. Why is this happening to me?

Then, on the way to school, my mate Des made me feel even worse.

"It's our swimming test today," he said. "Good job it isn't for real! If I really had to save someone, they'd drown!"

He laughed. I didn't.

Swimming!

That was the last thing I wanted to do right then.

While I was in bed, I had skipped in time to the fisherman's cottage. While I was in the freezing sea, I had skipped to the bathroom.

I knew what would happen. Miss would pick Des to save me. I would jump back in time again and, this time *I would drown.*

Soon, we were at the baths. I usually have a laugh with Des but today was different. Today, I just stared at the blue pool.

"Don't worry," said Des. "You're the best swimmer in the school!"

But I was stiff with fear.

First Samantha Butterworth saved Charlotte Foster. Then Claire Tinney saved Heather Matlock.

It was easy. The water was flat and
warm and only one metre deep.

Next Miss Finch pointed to Desmond.
"Save Daniel Sullivan."

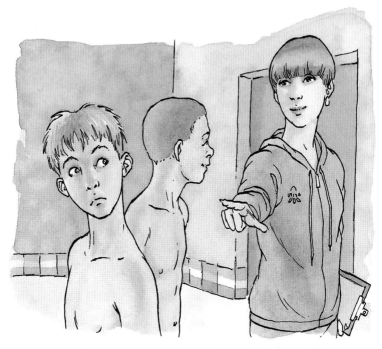

I should have run away right then. But,
instead, I slipped into the water.

One-two-three strokes later my arms
weighed tons. My head was sinking under
the water. The world was foggy and cold.
I was drowning.

"No, NO, NOOOO!" I spluttered.
I could just hear Herbert Ramsbottom
laughing out loud. "Hey! He's even
pretending to drown!"

"Up! Get up!" I told myself. With a
huge effort, I got my mouth clear.
"Grandad! Save me!" I yelled.
Now the class roared.
"HA! HA! HA! *Grandad!!!*"

Then I heard the thunder of the Sea of Darkness all around.

Suddenly strong arms snatched me up.

"By God, he's alive, Tobias! Michael's alive!"

Above were hard hands and hard faces. I was lying in the bottom of a boat.

"But Jem, I cannot see Point Cove. I fear we're all lost!" The rescuers were in trouble and so was I.

And then I felt the tiles at the side of the pool scraping my face. Somebody was thumping my back and I was coughing up water.

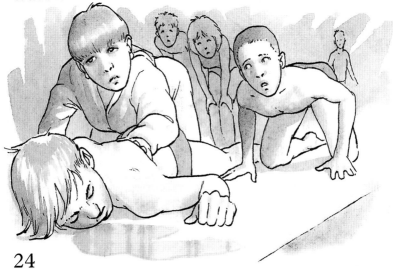

Back *at the baths* again!

"Daniel! Oh, *Daniel*! What *happened* to you?" Miss Finch's eyes were big with worry.

In the end, I wobbled to my feet.

"I think we'd better get you home!" said the teacher looking pale.

"But *it's not over yet*!" I yelled.

"Oh, yes, it is!" she said firmly. "You are *going home*!"

And that's what happened. Mum picked me up in the car. I was whisked off home and tucked up in bed.

Why is this happening to me? *Why?* I thought. If only I knew what it was all about.

Chapter Three

The next day, my Mum kept me off
school. The night had been quiet. There
was no sea, no boat in trouble, even in my
dreams. But I knew that couldn't last.

I tried to sort it out in my head. If I'm
me, how can I drown as Michael?

And also ... if the old fisherman thought
I was Michael, I must *look like Michael*.
And if I looked like Michael maybe he was
a member of my family long ago?

I wanted to ask Dad. He had books about the family, diaries and stuff like that. Trouble was, he was away in America for a whole month.

When Mum was busy, I had a look round Dad's study. There were books everywhere. Big books, small books, maps, charts.

What was I looking for? Something old,
something to do with the sea ... something
... hey! What was *that*?

At the end of a shelf was a black bundle.
A piece of string held it together. Now,
that looked old. I undid the string. It was
a bible, an old black bible. I took a sniff at
it – the *sea*! *A fisherman's bible!*

I tried to open it. Off came the front
cover.

UH! UH! Trouble? But not worse than
drowning!

What should I look for? The first page was as messy as the rest of the book. It looked like it had been in water.

Then I saw some faint writing.

It said *Michael Fletcher Sulli … b.1876 … grace … God … the sea … Point Cove.* Bits were washed out.

Michael! And the sea! 1876? That might be right for the old fisherman's cottage with no lights. *And,* the best clue of all – *Point Cove!*

Also, my dad's name is Roger Fletcher Sullivan. Mine is Daniel Fletcher Sullivan. In fact, all boys in my family have Fletcher as a middle name, I don't know why.

So this Michael *was* something to do with my family.

Now I knew it was all real. The only questions were: did Michael drown or not? And, if he did, would I drown too if I went back to being him?

"You still look a bit off, Danny," said my Mum at tea-time. "Will you be well enough to go to Point Cove with the school tomorrow?"

Point Cove!

Tomorrow!

BOOM! Suddenly it was all there in my mind.

Whatever it is, *it's going to happen tomorrow!* I thought, and I can't stop it!

Chapter Four

Next morning, we got to Point Cove early. Everyone was happy, ready for the fair. I felt weird.

Suddenly, I found myself walking away from the others. I was heading for Point Lighthouse.

Don't go that way! I told myself. Go to the fair! But my legs took no notice.

This is terrible, I thought. I'm trapped!
Trapped inside myself and nobody can
help me.

"Where are you going, man?" shouted
Des.

"Leave him, he's potty!"
called Marie.

Soon, I couldn't hear any sound at all.
No voices, no seagulls, no fair, not even
the sea.

My eyes were fixed on the church by the lighthouse. I could not look away even if I wanted to. There was no looking back, no turning back. My feet kept on walking.

What am I doing? I thought but on I went.

A moment later, my feet stopped.

I was in the graveyard. In front of me was a lonely stone by the sea wall. It said:

MICHAEL FLETCHER SULLIVAN

born 1876 died 1886

taken by the sea

GOD REST HIS SOUL

OH No! *Fletcher! That's us! That's me!* That's what was written in the bible! I should never have come here! *I'm going to drown!*

Then, little by little, the words misted over and the air grew cold and dark. Behind me the sea hissed and snarled and thundered. People on the beach were shouting.

I had another think. *I'm on the land. Michael's in the sea. That's* what I'm here for! *That's* why I keep going back in time – *to save Michael!*

Next thing, I was racing down the stony beach.

There, a group of people were pointing into the thundering water.

"What's happening?" one man asked.

"Out there are a dozen brave men," replied another. "Gone to save *Tobias Sullivan* and his grandson *Michael* from Reeper Rocks."

Off I went, storming into the monster waves. A stone's throw from the shore I could just see a boat's black shape. Suddenly, it rolled over like a great whale and out came the men.

There was no time to be afraid. No time to think.

Hang on Michael! I thought. *I'm coming!*

Dark figures swished by on the waves. They would be safe. But out there one small figure bounced in the swirl. No one else had seen him but me.

One minute he was there. The next he was gone.

Sometimes he bobbed. Sometimes he sank. Would I be in time?

By now the cold was getting to me.

WHOOSH! a great wave drove me under. Down I went, under the dark water.

Then WHAM! we were smashed together by the waves. I grabbed him tight but my head started to spin.

"Hold on! Hold on!" I croaked.

Slowly, slowly, in and in we crept towards the beach, sideways. Finally the rescuers snatched us from the sea. We fell, side by side, on to hard, cold stones.

I looked at Michael and he looked at me. For I was him and he was me. We looked so alike we might have been twins.

Suddenly Michael was hugged by his grizzly grandad.

"By heck, Michael. I thought you were gone!" the old man was crying.

And as he spoke, I turned back to the boy. There was so much to ask. So much to know.

But already it was all starting to fade away.

"Michael," I called. "Michael …!" but it was too late. He was gone and so was the crowd and the dark sea.

Seconds later, the sun was blinding me. And, out there, the sea was a shiny, golden mirror. I felt heavy, so very, very heavy but happy.

Far away the fairground was booming. Overhead the gulls were crying.

In the end, I wobbled up the cliff. But did I head for the fair?

No.

There was something I *had* to know.

Soon I was standing in front of the gravestone by the sea wall. But *now* it read:

MICHAEL FLETCHER SULLIVAN
born 1876 died **1941**
By the Grace of God
SAVED FROM THE SEA

Yes, Michael! We *made it*! I yelled and punched the air.

And I knew that it was all over and that the terrible Sea of Darkness was gone forever.

If you have enjoyed this book, why not try these other creepy titles:

The Claygate Hound by Jan Dean
It's the school trip to Claygate, and Zeb and Ryan are ready to explore, until they hear stories about the ghost in the woods. It all sounds like a stupid story. But then the boys start to see shadows moving in the trees and eyes glistening in the darkness. Could the Claygate Hound really exist?

The Ghosts of Golfhawk School by Tessa Potter
Martin and Dan like to scare others with stories about the ghosts at Golfhawk School. But when Kirsty arrives and strange things start to happen it no longer seems a joke. Can she really see ghostly figures in the playground? And why have students and teachers started to get sick?

Beware the Wicked Web by Anthony Masters
Where had the enormous, dusty spider's web come from? The sticky, silky folds had filled the attic room, and were now clinging to Rob and Sam as they explored the room. In the centre of the web was a huge egg, which was just about to hatch…

Time Flies by Mary Hooper
The large oak box looked like the perfect place to hide, but Lucy could never have imagined what powers lay inside. Lucy steps back in time to a strange and scary world. Can she find her way home again before it's too late?

Ghost on the Landing by Eleanor Allen
Jack wakes in the night screaming in fear. His sister's ghost stories about Aunt Stella's spooky old house must have been giving him nightmares. But was it just a bad dream or does the ghost on the landing really exist?